THE FIENDISH REVENGE OF LEROY JONES

THE FIENDISH REVENGE OF LEROY JONES

VIVIAN FRENCH

Illustrated by
KORKY PAUL

Barrington Stoke

For Ross Anderson, and all at
Preston Street Primary, Edinburgh,
with much love

First published in 2018 in Great Britain by
Barrington Stoke Ltd
18 Walker Street, Edinburgh, EH3 7LP

www.barringtonstoke.co.uk

Text © 2018 Vivian French
Illustrations © 2018 Korky Paul

The moral right of Vivian French and Korky Paul to be
identified as the author and illustrator of this work has been
asserted in accordance with the Copyright, Designs and
Patents Act, 1988

A CIP catalogue record for this book is available
from the British Library upon request

ISBN: 978-1-78112-826-8

Printed in China by Leo

CONTENTS

CHAPTER 1

A lie ... and the truth

Hi!

This is me.

My name is Leroy Jones, and I'm in my first year at Fairlawn High.

Sorry. That's a lie.

My name isn't Leroy. My mum went utterly bonkers when I was born. She called me Glorious Heavenly Baby Jones. Mad, or what?

I never tell anyone. It's my biggest secret. Would you believe my mum's PROUD of my name? She likes chatting to people, and she tells them how she chose a Very Special Name for a Very Special Baby. Then, when they find out what it is, they look at me as if I've dropped in from Outer Space.

Gah!

So it was my mum's fault that Amy Strundle ended up the way she did.

It wasn't my fault.

Well ... not much.

*

It all started on a Friday morning. I was walking out of assembly when Mr Mitchell pounced on me.

"Leroy Jones!" he yelled, and I jumped. "Come here!"

I tried to look as if I was in a huge hurry. "I've got maths, sir," I told him. "Got to dash!"

Mr Mitchell came closer. He wears glasses, and they make his big green eyes look like gooseberries. "Rubbish!" he said. "Now, listen to me. I've had a good idea, and you're the lad I need."

"Me, sir?" I said. "I don't think I am, sir. I'm no good at anything."

"Quite right," Mr Mitchell agreed. "Leroy Jones, school failure. But I don't like failures, Leroy. I want you to be a success! So I'm sending you out of school."

I blinked. Was I being expelled?

"You're going to be our school ambassador, Leroy," Mr Mitchell explained. "You, my boy, are going to spend three days at Hilltop Infants' School!" And he beamed at me as if he'd just given me the best present ever.

This was even worse than being expelled. Hilltop Infants was my old school, and I was being sent back there!

"Erm ..." I gulped. "Erm ..."

Mr Mitchell banged me on the back. "No need to thank me!" he said. "You'll have a ball, Leroy! You'll be helping the youngest children with their show for a special assembly. What an opportunity! And remember ... you'll be an ambassador for Fairlawn High. Wear your blazer, and make sure you look tidy. I'll be there to see the show, so don't let us down."

My head was spinning. A SPECIAL ASSEMBLY? What did I know about special assemblies? And I hated standing up in front of people. What if I had to be in it? But then I had a thought. Mr Mitchell said I was going to help the little ones.

I began to feel better. Small children would think I was really grown up. They'd do just

what I said. Maybe it wouldn't be too bad ...
and I'd have three whole days out of school.

CHAPTER 2

Amy Strundle ...
and why she hated me

On Monday morning I was halfway down the road before I remembered I was meant to be going to Hilltop Infants. I swung round, and headed off in the right direction. I was almost there when I heard someone shouting my name ... and my heart almost jumped out of my chest.

It was Amy Strundle.

*

I need to tell you about Amy Strundle. She was in my class at junior school, and she hated me. Why? I don't know.

Well ... it might have been because she fell over my feet in the dinner hall when we were in year three. She had a tray full of food, and she ended up on the floor with her face in her treacle pudding and custard. She said I tripped her, but I promise I didn't! I didn't even laugh, not like some people. She wasn't looking where she was going – everyone said so, but Amy didn't believe them.

After that she picked on me non-stop, and I was SO HAPPY when I heard she was going to a different high school.

I had thought I'd never see her again.

But now Amy was yelling at me from across the road. "Bat ears!" she shouted. "Bum face! Widdle pants! What are YOU doing here?"

I decided I'd try to take no notice of her. I marched towards the school gates ... and she followed me.

"I asked you a question, weasel nose!" Amy screeched. "Got egg in your ears?"

I was at the main school door. Safety! I rang the bell.

"I'm helping here," I told Amy, and I waited for the school secretary to come and rescue me.

"WHAT?" Amy's eyes bulged. "You too?"

My stomach flipped, and I felt as if I'd swallowed an ice lolly. "Are you ... are you going to be here as well?" I asked.

"I'm helping the kiddie widdies," Amy told me. "I'm good at that stuff, me. Not like you, mummy's pet." Then her eyes gleamed, and she looked so pleased with herself. She was like a hungry python that had spotted a baby rabbit. "Hey! Guess what!" she went on. "My mum met your mum the other day. They had SUCH a nice chat, and you'll never guess what I found out!"

"What—" I began, but at that moment someone opened the door. It was Mrs Barker, my old teacher, and she smiled at us.

"Leroy and Amy!" Mrs Barker said. "You're here! The class are so excited! They've got lots of wonderful ideas – and they can't wait to tell you all about them. I'll take you to the hall first, and introduce you to the children. We've just finished assembly."

Mrs Barker led us off down the corridor, chatting as she went. Amy walked next to her, and I trailed behind.

'This is going to be the worst week of my life,' I thought. A whole three days of Amy Strundle! And what had she found out? I had a bad feeling that I already knew ...

CHAPTER 3

I'm not Uncle Gordon ...

The school hall was smaller than I remembered it. There was a new head teacher, Mrs Jindal, and she was very bright and bouncy. She skipped up to meet us, clapping her hands.

The little kids were sitting in rows on the floor, and they stared at me and Amy as if we were aliens. I thought they looked pretty weird as well. Small and squeaky. Like hamsters.

"Look, children!" Mrs Jindal said. "Our helpers have arrived! Aren't we lucky?" Mrs Jindal pointed to Amy. "This is Amy! Say good morning to Amy, everyone!"

The kids chanted, "Good morning, Amy," and Amy waved at them.

Mrs Jindal twirled round to me. "And this is our other helper ... oh goodness! I've forgotten his name!"

I opened my mouth to tell her, but Mrs Jindal hushed me. "Shh!" she said. "We'll play a game. Who can guess our new friend's name?"

A small boy put his hand up. He had paint on his nose and all over his jumper. "Uncle Gordon."

Mrs Jindal smiled at him. "Oh, Troy!" she said. "What a wonderful suggestion. But I don't think that's quite right. Would someone else like to try?"

This time an older girl stuck up her hand and said, "Spotty Mouse."

"No, Sophie, dear," Mrs Jindal told her. "Not Spotty Mouse. Let's have one last try."

"You'll never guess," Amy said, and began to giggle. I looked at her, and I was worried. Did Amy know? That bad feeling was back again ...

"He's called Glorious Heavenly Baby Jones!" Amy was laughing so much she nearly fell over, and all the kids began to laugh as well. And then she began to sing.

"Glorious Heavenly Baby Jones,
"Shakes his head and rattles his bones!"

Amy was really enjoying herself. She pranced round the room, shaking her head, and the kids went wild. They rolled about on the floor, and they shouted,

"Baby Jones! Rattle his bones!"

I thought Mrs Jindal would clap her hands and tell Amy to stop, but she didn't. She was laughing almost as much as the little kids, and so were the other teachers.

I had to stand there, my face getting redder and redder. I wanted the floor to open and swallow me up. Even more, I wanted Amy to feel as stupid and embarrassed as I did.

But I had no idea how to do it.

I needed a plan.

A plan to get my revenge.

CHAPTER 4

My special name ...

It took at least five minutes for everyone to calm down.

Of course, Amy didn't help. She kept giggling, and that set the little kids off again.

At long last they were quiet, and Mrs Jindal smiled. "I can see why they sent you here, Amy," she said. "We love jokes in our school." She pointed to a big poster on the wall. It said, "Laughter and fun helps our work get done."

Mrs Jindal turned to me and asked, "So what's your real name?"

"Leroy Jones," I said, but Amy wasn't going to let me away with that.

"His real name's Glorious, Miss." Amy grinned. "Cross my heart and hope to die! Glorious Heavenly Baby Jones!"

Mrs Jindal looked very surprised. "Is that true?" she asked me.

I nodded, and Mrs Jindal coughed. I could tell she was a bit embarrassed. "That's a very ... erm ... special name," she said. "Do all your family have names like that?"

"No," I said.

That was a lie, but I wasn't going to start telling her about my weird hippy mother (Suzi Silver Starburst) or my weird kid sister (Pipsi Petal Golden Girl). I sneaked a look at Amy to see if she was going to say anything, but she didn't.

"I can't help it if I've got a 'special name',"
I said. I knew I sounded grumpy, but I didn't
care. "And I like being called Leroy."

"Now, now, Leroy!" Mrs Jindal gave me
a dazzling smile. "Turn that frown upside
down! We don't like cross faces here in Hilltop
Infants!" She clapped her hands again. "Time
to go to our classrooms. Tia, will you show
Amy the way, please? And, Angelo, will you
show Leroy?"

A tiny girl with her hair in tufts jumped up.
"I'm Tia," she said. "We go this way," and she
led Amy out of the hall.

Angelo stayed sitting down. "I don't want
to," he said. "I don't like him."

Mrs Jindal gave a trill of laughter. "Oh,
Angelo! What a funny boy you are! Zak, will
you show Leroy where to go?"

Zak got up. "This way," he said, and he took my hand. His hand was very sticky, and he smelled of strawberry jam. He had toast crumbs on his jumper, and what looked like butter in his hair. I wondered if he'd eaten his breakfast, or rolled in it.

CHAPTER 5

When a frog got squashed ...

When I was in infant school, we had to sit at tables. This classroom was full of big bean bags, and the tables were right at the back. The walls were covered in messy paintings, and so many things were hanging from the ceiling I couldn't even see what colour it was.

The teacher was called Miss Denny, and she was very tall. She was wearing lots of floaty scarves, and she did a skip of happiness when we came in. She wasn't at all like the teachers I knew. I saw Amy rolling her eyes, and for once I agreed with her.

"My angels!" Miss Denny said, and she rushed to meet us. For an awful moment I thought she was going to hug me. I ducked out of the way, and trod on something ... something crunchy.

"WAAAAAAAAAAH!"

I spun round, and saw a little girl yelling her head off. A squashed plastic frog lay on the floor beside her.

"You've deaded my froggie!" the little girl shouted. She ran at me, and kicked me as hard as she could.

"Ouch!" I clutched my leg. What was I meant to do? I was pretty sure I wasn't meant to kick her back.

Amy was laughing so much she could hardly stand up. "You're meant to kiss frogs, not squash them!" she told me.

Miss Denny scooped up the little girl, and gave me a cold stare. "Poor Pansy! Please tell her you're sorry you hurt her frog."

My leg hurt a lot, but I muttered, "Sorry, Pansy. I didn't mean to break your frog."

Pansy leaned out of Miss Denny's arms. "You're a horrid boy!" she squeaked. "I don't like you."

I nearly told Pansy I didn't like her much, too, but I didn't.

Amy was still giggling. "You've got feet like plates of meat, Glorious Heavenly Baby! Great big feet, plates of meat!"

Pansy began to giggle too. "Babies don't have meaty feet!"

"This one does," Amy told her, and then both of them were laughing.

"Clever Amy." Miss Denny was pleased. "You've really cheered Pansy up. Now, we've got lots to do today. We need to make all our masks for our special assembly ... we're going to tell the story of Noah's Ark. OH!" She clapped her hands, and she had the same mad look that Mr Mitchell gets when he has a Good Idea. My heart sank. That look always means trouble.

"I've had SUCH a clever idea," Miss Denny said. "Leroy and Amy – you can be Mr and Mrs Noah! You can read the story while the children act it out."

"I'd LOVE to, Miss Denny!" Amy said, and she smiled a huge smile. If you'd seen her then, you'd have thought she was the nicest, sweetest girl in the whole wide world. She went on, "And Leroy will be a cute Mr Noah, won't you, Leroy?"

Amy wasn't being nice or sweet at all. She knew how much I hate standing up in front of people. I hate the feeling of loads of eyes peering at me. And, most of all, I really, REALLY hate reading out loud.

"Do I have to?" I asked. "I'd much rather make things. I'd like to help make the masks. And the ark."

Miss Denny pretended to look sad. "Oh, Leroy!" she said. "Please don't let us down. Noah's lovely little animals need you."

"But I'm no good at reading," I said. I SO didn't want to do it.

"Amy can help you," Miss Denny said as she patted Amy's arm. "I'm sure Mrs Noah did most of the talking, and Amy's got a lovely clear voice. But we really must get busy. We need to make all the masks by the end of today ... and tomorrow we'll make the ark."

The little kids went to the back of the room, and Amy and I went with them. Amy took my arm as if we were friends, and then she pinched me hard. I tried not to yell, as I knew that was what she wanted, but it wasn't easy.

There were heaps of paper and card and coloured tissue on the tables. There were also plastic scissors, tubes of glue, and paint and brushes.

Zak rushed to a table. "I want to make a mask," he said. "Me and Angelo, we want to be Storm Troopers!"

"I don't think Mr Noah had Storm Troopers on the Ark, Zak," Miss Denny said. "What animal would you like to be?"

"I don't want to be an animal." Angelo stuck out his lower lip. "I want to be a Storm Trooper!"

Miss Denny gave a weak smile. "Very well," she said. "Leroy – would you like to help Angelo and Zak?"

"And me! And me! And me!" lots of kids shouted, and they started jumping up and down. "We want to be Storm Troopers!"

"Goodness!" Miss Denny said. She looked at me. "I'll put you in charge, Leroy. I don't know much about Storm Troopers."

CHAPTER 6

The stickiness of glue ...

That was when I found out that five year olds can't use scissors. Also, school scissors are useless. The plastic can't cut anything! I had to do the cutting-out with Miss Denny's normal metal pair.

I made three masks, and I thought I was doing OK. But then Billie dropped a tube of glue. Before I could pick it up, Amy slid across from the next table and stepped on it. Glue shot out over my trousers and shoes.

"Oh, Leroy," Amy squealed. "Look what you've done. You've trodden on the glue!"

"I didn't – you did," I said, but it wasn't any good.

Miss Denny came over, took a look at my shoes, and of course she believed Amy.

"Really, Leroy!" Miss Denny sounded cross. "You need to be more careful."

"Sorry," I muttered. I could see Amy smiling with glee.

'Just you wait, Amy Strundle,' I thought. 'Sooner or later, I'll get my own back on you ...'

As I thought about revenge, Angelo, Zak and Billie were having a lovely time pretending they were stuck to the floor.

"Ooooh! I'll be here for ever and ever!" Billie yelled. "I'll be here till Christmas!"

"Look, miss!" Angelo waved his arms madly. "We can't move!"

And then all the other kids jumped into the mess and pretended they were stuck too.

Miss Denny wasn't pleased. Not at all.

It took a lot of mopping before I got the floor clean again. Amy sat and grinned while I puffed and panted and scrubbed. I'd almost

finished when I saw her pick up the pot of red paint. I was sure I knew what she was going to do ...

And I was right. Amy tipped the paint over, and I had to start again.

The rest of the day wasn't too bad. Well ... just as long as I didn't think about having to read in the special assembly. Miss Denny asked Amy to put elastic string on the masks, and then the kids started to make ears and tails. My group still wanted to be Storm Troopers, so I made a suggestion.

"How about if you're *animal* Storm Troopers?" I said.

The kids grumbled a bit, but then they said yes, so we set to work. It took me ages, but it kept me away from Amy. Angelo wanted to be a tiger, and Zak did too. Billie wanted to be an elephant. We made those, and then we made three monkeys, a giraffe, and a hippo. I thought the masks looked quite good, and so did Miss Denny. She gave me a proper smile and said, "Well done, Leroy!"

Amy snorted, but she didn't say anything.

But I saw the nasty look in her eyes. When the bell rang for the end of school, I didn't leave with Amy. I hid in the toilets until she was gone.

That night, I lay awake for a long time trying to dream up ways to get my revenge, but it wasn't any good. I couldn't think of anything that would work.

I decided to see what happened the next day. Maybe I'd have an idea then?

CHAPTER 7

Why I was late for school ...

The next day started badly.

My idiot kid sister Pipsi had drawn spots and squiggles all over her arms with a black marker pen, and Mum couldn't clean it off. Pipsi was screaming because she thought they'd be cross with her at nursery. Mum was yelling that it was her own silly fault.

When I saw it was MY pen, I started shouting as well, so Mum told me off for leaving it around. I couldn't find my pencil case, so I shoved the pen in my blazer pocket. And then

Mum sent me to the corner shop to buy some baby wipes, and of course there was a queue ...

So I was late getting to Hilltop Infants.

Miss Denny wasn't thrilled when I arrived after the bell had gone. "I'm disappointed, Leroy," she said.

I thought of telling her why I was late, but decided it wasn't worth it. "I'm really sorry, miss," I said.

"Make sure you're on time tomorrow," Miss Denny snapped. "Our special assembly is at ten, and we need to be ready."

I didn't need to be reminded. I was dreading having to stand up and read in front of everyone.

Amy was sitting at a table with a group of little kids. She had a super smug look on her face. "I told Miss Denny how you're always late for everything," she said.

That was SO not true. I glared at Amy, but she pretended not to see. She was helping the kids colour in their animal masks. Most of them were finding it hard, and Amy wasn't much better. In fact, she was worse.

I watched Amy scribbling over the lines and using the wrong colours. It was awful. I felt so sorry for the kids, and I didn't know what to do. If a crocodile had walked in and tried to eat Amy for his dinner, I wouldn't have stopped him. I love drawing and making things, and I hate seeing people make a mess.

I took a deep breath and asked Amy, "Do you want me to help?"

"Get lost, bat ears," she hissed.

"Bat ears!" Pansy said. "She called him bat ears!" And she jumped up and down, giggling madly.

Miss Denny gave Amy a cross look.

"Amy, that's not kind," she said. "We don't call people names here, do we, boys and girls?"

"No, Miss Denny," the children said in the funny sing-song way that little kids always talk.

Miss Denny nodded. "That's right. And what do we do if we forget?"

"Say sorry," the kids chanted.

Amy looked so horrified I almost burst out laughing.

"Ermmmm," Amy muttered. "Sorry."

If looks could kill, I'd have been dead as a door nail from the stare Amy gave me.

"Thank you, Amy," Miss Denny said. "And now, let's get busy. We have an ark to build! Leroy, I'm relying on you for this. Tia, Amma, Zak and Billie can help you. Everyone else, come with me and Amy, and we'll sort out your costumes."

And with that, Miss Denny swept Amy up to the other end of the classroom.

It was hard not to cheer. But I didn't. I kept my face very serious.

Then I sat my helpers down so we could design the best ark ever. We had six huge cardboard boxes, and I knew we could make something brilliant.

CHAPTER 8

A beautiful ark ...

I enjoyed myself working with the kids and
the boxes. Even better, Amy was kept busy
all morning. She spilled a glass of water on
me at break, but nothing else. I heard her ask
Miss Denny if she could help with the ark, but
Miss Denny said no.

Perhaps Miss Denny had seen that Amy and
I were at war with each other?

Billie, Tia, Zak and Amma turned out to
be great at cutting and sticking. Soon the ark
began to look amazing. By lunch time we'd
almost finished – it just needed painting.

"Well done, Team Leroy!" Miss Denny said, and gave us all a high five. "That's fantastic. You've done a great job!"

After lunch, Amma asked if we could start to paint the ark.

"I think we should let some other children have a turn," Miss Denny said. "And Amy says she'd like a go. Leroy, could you tidy up the book cupboard for me? I've been wanting someone neat to do that all term."

I told Miss Denny I'd be happy to, but inside I was thinking, 'Oh no! Not my beautiful ark! Amy will ruin it!'

I was right. When I got back from sorting the books into neat rows, Amy and her team had sloshed all kinds of colours on the cardboard ark. They'd drawn silly big-eyed rabbits on the roof, and love hearts on the doors.

Love hearts! On an ARK!!

Miss Denny didn't say it was a mess, but nor did she say it was good. She said it was "very cheerful".

Amy gave me a sly smile. "We tried to make it nice," she said. "But it won't stand up properly. Leroy isn't as clever as he thinks he is, Miss Denny. The ark keeps falling over."

"No, it doesn't," I said, and I went round to the back of the ark. When I got there, I saw Amy had cut the supports … so she was right. The ark wouldn't stand up by itself any more.

I was so angry I almost exploded. "What did you do that for?" I asked Amy. "You've ruined it!"

Amy shrugged. "Those old bits of cardboard? They were in the way."

Miss Denny came to look. "Oh dear," she said. "Oh dear, oh dear."

Amy put on her Good Girl Face. "I'm ever so sorry, miss. I didn't think those bits mattered."

I stood and looked at the damage some more.

And I had a sudden mega-genius idea.

"If someone sits behind the ark, they can hold it up," I said. "They can open and shut the doors as well. I can do that, miss!" Then I tried to look sad. "It would mean I can't be Mr Noah ..."

CHAPTER 9

A strange collection of animals ...

For a terrible moment I thought Miss Denny was going to say no. There was a spare box I could have used to make more supports for the ark ... Luckily for me, she didn't notice.

"Very well, Leroy," Miss Denny said. "That's kind of you. Amy can be Mrs Noah, and I'll be Mr Noah. We'll read the story between us."

I tried not to show how pleased I was. No reading out loud! 'Well played, Leroy Jones,' I told myself.

We went over the play in the school hall for the rest of the afternoon. I had one of the small chairs to sit on behind the ark. I opened and shut the cardboard doors to let in the animals ... and I was very helpful.

Pansy was the dove, but she never could remember when to fly out. It was lucky I was there to give her a push every time.

Amy stood at one side of the stage to read the story, and Miss Denny was on the other. We had a blue sheet for the water, flapped about by two bigger kids. When the water began to rise, Amy led the animals into the ark. Then, when Pansy the dove came back with her green leaf, Amy led the animals back out again.

By the end of the day everyone knew what they were meant to be doing ... more or less.

The tigers kept pushing in front of the elephants, and the hippo was cross because he had to walk with the giraffe. (Nobody wanted

to be the second hippo, or the second giraffe.)
There were three monkeys not two, an awful
lot of Storm Troopers, two mermaids and a
rainbow unicorn ...

But otherwise we were ready for the special
assembly.

I'm not sure what the real Mr and Mrs Noah would have thought of our collection of animals, but Miss Denny said they were all wonderful. I saw she was looking very tired.

Amy had been enjoying being important so much she'd almost forgotten about picking

on me. But not quite. She'd made sure she
stepped on my feet every time she came into
the ark. Then, when nobody was looking, she'd
pinched my nose so hard she'd made my eyes
water.

"Ooooh, look! The Glorious Baby's crying!"
she'd sneered, but then she had to go back on
stage so she couldn't do anything else mean.

I had blown my nose, and done some hard
thinking. I was running out of time if I was
going to get my revenge. I needed an idea ...
and I needed one fast.

CHAPTER 10

Squiggles and spots ...

When I got home that evening, my kid sister Pipsi was sulking in the kitchen. Her arms were bright red, and still covered in squiggles and spots.

"Everyone laughed at me at nursery," she moaned. "Mrs Nair put special cream on me to make the pen go away, but it didn't work. And Mum made my arms hurt."

"It'll be OK soon," I said. I wanted to say she shouldn't have helped herself to my stuff, but I didn't. She looked too unhappy.

Mum sighed. "I had a look online," she told me, "and it said nail polish remover gets rid of marker pen – but it made Pipsi's skin so sore I couldn't use it. She'll just have to wait until it fades."

"Poor old Pipsi," I said. Then I asked, "Mum – what would you do if you wanted to get revenge on a bully?"

"Revenge?" Mum said, shocked. "That's a horrid idea. If you're being bullied, you should tell me – or a teacher. Who's bullying you?"

"No one. It doesn't matter," I said. I wanted to deal with this myself. Mum would just make it worse. "It's not me who's being bullied," I lied.

"Well, whoever it is should tell someone," Mum said. "And perhaps they could try making friends with the bully. Deep down, most bullies are very unhappy, and lonely."

"I don't think this bully is," I said. "I think she's one hundred per cent horrible, from the top of her head to the end of her toes."

"Oh dear." Mum shook her head, and then she looked thoughtful. "My mother always told me revenge was a dish best served cold."

"What does that mean?" I asked.

"It means you shouldn't rush into anything while you're angry," Mum said. "You should think carefully, and make a plan. Now, come and eat your tea while it's hot."

I sighed.

I should have guessed my mother wouldn't be any help with my revenge plans.

The next day I got to Hilltop Infants early. I was a bit nervous about the play – but at least I didn't have to read or say anything now. Miss

Denny seemed pleased to see me, and so did Tia and Zak and Billie and Amma – they rushed over to give me a hug. I didn't mind being hugged by them. It felt kind of nice.

When Amy arrived she was carrying a big bag.

"I've got a costume," she said. "And I've been thinking. I want to be Mr Noah, not Mrs Noah. After all, it's me who leads the animals into the ark."

Miss Denny nodded. "If you like, Amy."

Amy pulled a brown dressing gown out of the bag, and put it on. "There," she said. "It's perfect for Mr Noah, isn't it? And I've got a head-dress too."

She did. It was a stripy tea towel, and it looked good. But I wasn't going to tell Amy that.

"AND I've got my mum's black eyeliner, so I can give myself a beard," Amy added. "I'm going to be the star of the show!"

CHAPTER 11

The story of Noah's Ark ...

All the kids were wild with excitement that morning.

Another teacher came to help our class, and he and Miss Denny stuffed everyone into their costumes. I sorted out the masks. Amy was no help at all. She was too busy prancing about in her dressing gown and tea towel.

"Amy ... are you ready?" Miss Denny asked. She sounded almost cross.

"I've got to put on my make-up first," Amy said, as if she was a real actress. She flumped down on my chair behind the ark, and handed me a mirror. "Hold that, bat ears," she ordered. She fished in her pocket, and pulled out something that looked like a pen. "Now for my beard." She giggled. "My mum will kill me when she finds out I've taken it. It's a dead posh eyeliner!"

Amy twisted at the pen, but she couldn't get it open. "Here! You do it!" she said. She handed the pen to me, and grabbed the mirror.

The pen had a fiddly cap, and I had a hard time with it too. While I tugged at it, Amy made faces at herself in the mirror – pouting and smiling. She wasn't watching as I tried to twist the eyeliner open. But when my marker pen fell out of my blazer pocket, she jumped.

"Don't drop it, bum face!" she hissed. Then she snatched up my pen, and pulled off the cap.

So what should I have done?

Told Amy she'd made a mistake?

Or kept quiet?

I was still trying to make up my mind when Amy crossed her eyes and sneered at me. "You're useless, widdle pants! Hold my mirror, and don't move!"

That was it.

I didn't say anything as she drew all over her face with the marker pen. On went a moustache, and a beard, and thick black eyebrows.

I did wonder how she'd feel when the play was over. And how she'd feel when she went back to her normal school the next day.

I wouldn't be there to see, but I didn't mind. Just thinking about it made me smile.

"What are you grinning at, bat ears?" Amy demanded.

I shrugged, and a moment later the grans and grandpas and mums and dads and friends started to arrive. Miss Denny told Amy to go to the side of the stage, and I sat down in my chair ... still smiling.

So what happened?

We managed to tell the story of Noah's Ark. The tigers had a fight with the elephant, and then the three monkeys joined in, but it didn't last long. The mermaids got splinters from sliding about on the floor, and the unicorn's horn fell off. Pansy the dove forgot to come back with her green leaf until Miss Denny hissed at her ... but all the people watching loved every second.

They clapped and cheered for ages.

Then Miss Denny stood up and asked everyone to thank her splendid helpers,

Leroy Jones and Amy Strundle. She said the wonderful ark was down to me, and everyone cheered. Amy looked furious. But Mr Mitchell looked really proud. He was sitting in the front row, and he clapped very loudly.

And then it was all over ...

And Amy went to the toilets to wash her face.

I didn't wait to hear her scream. I was on my way home.

So that's my story. I'll sign out now ...

The gloriously happy Leroy Jones.

P.S. I think what my mum said was true. Revenge really is a dish best served cold.

P.P.S. When I got home that day, Pipsi was clean again. My mum had found out coconut oil gets rid of marker pen. Of course, it was too late to tell Amy. What a shame!

Our books are tested
for children and young people by
children and young people.

Thanks to everyone who consulted on
a manuscript for their time and effort in
helping us to make our books better
for our readers.